TO OUR BOYS.

From George Emmett, Greeting :—

Boys, you have my Comic Annual; it is the first of the kind and price yet published. Next year no doubt a dozen will be submitted to you, for there is much imitation in these days, and the ways of your old friend are even now being deftly plagiarized, and his old dishes are being hashed up as novelties—but no matter, the time will come, &c., and so forth.

Boys, I am as tired as you are of the old Christmas numbers, so I called a special meeting of the Hogarth House staff, including Dabber, who by the way is very wroth at a counterfeit Dabber being brought forth—

"Wot's the use," he said, when I asked him to visit the Spiritualists, "Wot's the use ? them as ain't got brains must keep me and my brains. Sure as I go I'll be irritated by 'em."

I soothed the friend of "Nelsing;" told him to take a bottle of rum in his starboard pocket. The soothing and the rum succeeded, especially the rum, and a five pound note, and "Nelsing's" friend went on his way. What occurred we will relate in this Annual.

"Philander," I said to that enterprising youth, "You must visit a skating rink; take your pencil, Philander, and let our boys have a graphically illustrated account of your experience on the rink."

"Sir," said Philander, "I will go upon one condition, and that condition I must whisper to you."

Philander whispered.

Yours obediently started with surprise, looked very blue, then desperately dived in a pocket, brought forth a pocket-book—there followed a chink of golden pieces as Philander extended his palm.

Philander and Dabber's plan was nobly followed by the staff; the stout pocket-book became a mere shadow, yours to command fell backward in a chair, and as the last of the staff left the door, I flung an old ledger after the manly form.

Now, boys, what do you think of our joint efforts? Does it please you? If so, tell your chums that

GEORGE EMMETT'S COMIC ANNUAL

can be bought everywhere, for One Penny. If you don't like it, don't buy another next year. Whether or not, we wish you a

"Jolly Christmas, a Lucky New Year, and all the Good you could wish Yourselves."

Ring up the Curtain, Please !

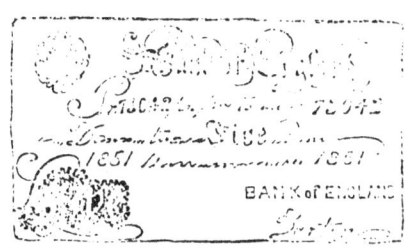

FROM CORNEY DABBER TO ALL THE YOUNG'UNS WHO READS THIS BOOK.

YOUNG Britons, Sons of Britannias, and Young Hinglishmens, has a shoman I makes my bow to yer all. This is a wenture. Mr. Hemit wants ter say the notion wuss 'is, but don't none of yer beleve him. The hidea is mine, and I sez let him put his name on the frunt for a chee.* Wot do yer think the meen kus did? He didn't send me a chee, but a bank-note with a fotygraf on it;† "but" sez he in his letter, "Dabber, you're alwis losin' yure chees, so I sends a note wot hive had fotygrafed, so as it can be trased hef yew lose it." That's the fotygraf at the top of this page; I put it in fust ef all to hexpose Mr. Hemit's meenniss, and, secondly, becos that Filander miten't sneke it.

Filander's meen ernuf to sneke anything; hive knowed him to sneke a babby's shuger rag, and a chap wot wud be gilty ef that, wud sneke his granmother's corfin nales. He cum inter my room the hother day, and seeing a chee on the table he put out his 'and, but I stops him with a rap hover the nuckles.

"No, yer don't," sez I. "I want ter keep this one; yu've had too many ef my chees."

He tried to be cheaky, but it wudn't do, so he cum down and sez :—

"Dabber, don't be 'ard on a chap, now yure hup in the world. Lend us a tanner, and don't say nothin' more about it."

But no, I skorned the akt; a feller as wood thef a pore old woden-leged man's chee, warn't wurthy o' bein' helped, but sumowe, wen I looked at 'is hungry fase I hadn't got it in me hart tew deny, sow I give him the tanner and sez,—

"Filander, I'm agoin' to start a sho', leastways a hanual for Mr. Hemit, and I kan put a job in yer way hif yer like tew go in for it."

"Dabber," ses he with teers o' gratetude in his hies, "me aid you? We alwis been frien's,‡ say wot it is, and I'll do it."

"Wel, Filander," I ses skornful-like, because I knowed he was ony snekin' round me, "this hanual hime agoin' to start for Mr. Hemit is the best ef the kind hever dun, and it ell be a buster; next yere there might be severel hoppishuns, but me and Mr. Hemit is the starters ef this style ef book, and we orter hav the glory ef it."

"Braveho, Dabber!" he showtes, "I alwis knowed yer wus a man ef talent, and I'll stick by yer."

"Shet hup," sez I, for I knowed it wus ony blarney, "besides this hanual hime agoin', tew hev a sho'."

Then 'e wanted to kis my 'and, but I were that disgusted, that I were obliged to leeve 'im and get some refreshment. That's the sort of man Phil Jackson is.

---

* The ancient fibber's audacity is only to be equalled by his want of veracity.—ED.

† We had him over this transaction. His unsatisfactory account of the loss of the numerous cheques he has extorted from us of late has been anything but profitable. The photograph of the bank-note is no doubt a check on his fraudulent practices.—ED.

---

‡ Apart, Kilkenny cats are not more dangerous when together.

OUR BREAK-UP.

IT'S not much of a story, boys; it's more of a lesson to you than anything else. A lesson to speak out and speak plain, and I wish we had done so at the time.

It was our break-up at Christmas time. We were at school at Margate, and the Doctor, our master, told us he would travel with us as far as Herne Hill. Here the train divides, one portion goes to Victoria Station the other

"Old fool, old fool, eh! Wait until you return to school."

We had forgotten all about it by the time we returned. It is so jolly, you know, being home for the holidays.

The first morning before lessons the Doctor asked Tom Atkins to stand out.

Tom did so.

"Turn round," said the Doctor.

"ALL FULL, ALL FULL!" YELLED THE BOYS. "OLD FOOL, OLD FOOL, OLD FOOL, EH!" SAID THE DOCTOR; "WAIT UNTIL YOU RETURN TO SCHOOL.

half to Ludgate Hill. We, that is, the carriage full of boys, were booked for Victoria.

When we reached Herne Hill, the Doctor, after shaking hands all round, alighted from our carriage for the purpose of changing into the Ludgate Hill portion of the train.

He stood on the platform in the centre of a pile of luggage, and as the train moved off we shouted out,

"All full—all full—all full."

I don't know why we shouted.. Tom Atkins, leaning out of the carriage window, began. Tom was always an ass and always will be.

The Doctor misunderstood us, for he shook his hand angrily, and said,

Tom turned round, and as he received a swinger from the master's open hand he sprang forward and gave a yell.

The Doctor could hit no end of hard 'uns.

I began to feel in a funk, for as Tom went away smoothing the seat of his trousers, the Doctor said,

"Old fool, eh! old fool!"

I tried to explain the mistake, but no go; in fact, it was worse for me, for I was kept to the last and received two open handers.

MORAL.

This Christmas I don't say a word when the Doctor leaves us at Herne Hill Station.

MISS FANNY'S FAN;

OR, CUPID ON WHEELS.

VERY likely you have heard of me. I am the real, original, and unadulterated Philander Jackson, H.U.A., the hero of a thousand fights, and the author of as many stories.

Fortune and I am not friends, and Fate, with all the viciousness of my boot-laces, takes a delight in tripping me up.

I do not murmur, Mr. Editor; I covet not

True, I was in the pit, and the eyes and fan in the dress boxes, but the moment I saw them this poor heart of mine went to work like a chronometer, and ever since it has ticked, increasing in speed to the power and vigour of a double-barrelled American clock.

As soon as the curtain descended on the last act I rushed into the street, determined to catch a full view of the face which the fan had partly hidden.

People jostled me as I stood. I hovered round the door. Policemen shoved and cursed me, but I stuck to my post.

My face turned the colour of a boiled lobster, and my heart gave a great bound as I saw that fan coming out.

gold, silver, or precious stones; I can laugh at adversity, and feel cheerful even at the fact of my uncle's borrowing my best coat every Monday and returning it on Saturday evening; but oh! it is sad to be the victim of unrequited love.

*   *   *   *   *

I have been compelled to leave off writing and roll in convulsions on the sofa, and I take up the pen again with trembling fingers and a throbbing brain.

Be still my heart; rest perturbed spirit, and let me tell the story of my woes.

It was at the theatre I first beheld a pair of blue eyes peeping over a white silk fan, spangled with dots of silver.

Heavens, what a face it concealed! White and as pure as alabaster was its complexion, a small, delicately-shaped nose, a dimpled chin, and a rosy little mouth, displaying two rows of pearly teeth.

I stood entranced !

I flushed red to my noble brow, and I became conscious that my hands, tied and spellbound to the sides of my legs, were working like a pair of crabs in a fishmonger's basket.

Do not blame me for what I am about to confess.

I saw this goddess enter a cab, and I followed, yes, followed it, to the very door of one of my dearest friends, and half-an-hour afterwards I sat next to Miss Fanny Lovelace at the supper table.

I believe I ate and drank something, but what or how much I cannot tell, but I have some dim idea that I emptied more than one plate of cold fowl, bones and all.

I know that I was the focus of all eyes, and perhaps they took me for a cannibal ; it may be so, but I only know that I was extremely happy and head-over-heels in love with the Fan and Miss Fanny.

Miss Lovelace was in a very lively mood. She talked and laughed gaily, rapped me over my knuckles and bridge of my nose until tears of mingled rapture and anguish poured from my eyes. The Fan was never out of sight, it was a kind of Will-o'-the-Wisp and guided me like some poor benighted traveller to my destruction.

"Do you rink much ?" Miss Lovelace asked, poking a corner of silver spangled white silk into the corner of my left eye.

I thought her question was, "Do you drink much," and fearing that I had in someway committed myself with the decanters, I became very stiff and dignified in an instant.

"Miss Lovelace," I said coldly, feeling as hot as a furnace myself, and conscious that the tip of my nose was as bright as a copper button, "I am almost a teetotaller."

"La !" cried Fanny, disturbing my favourite curl with her confounded fan. "What a funny man you must be. Are you a little deaf."

"Deaf, no ?" I echoed in a voice which might have chilled an iceberg. "Thanks be to Providence, I have all my faculties."

"I asked you if you rinked much," Fanny said, with a merry little giggle, "and you replied that you were almost a teetotaller."

I saw my mistake now, but I, the proud son of a Jackson and an H.U.A. into the bargain, did not intend to acknowledge it, so curling my moustache I said in a bantering tone—

"One must be steady on one's legs whilst rinking Miss Lovelace, and who so steady as a total abstainer ?"

"Who dares to talk of legs in the company of ladies ?" demanded a fat female at the bottom of the table. "Mr. Jackson, oblige me by changing the topic."

Up went the white ribbed silk and spangles, and Fanny's voice whispered from behind them, "Don't mind mamma, she's getting old and crotchety."

I felt that some explanation was due, and I having done so, pacified the old lady that she smiled so gracefully on me, and ogled me to such an extent, that I felt inclined to disappear under the table.

Mrs. Lovelace was a widow, and I averted her gaze, and trembled in my boots.

"I want to go to the rink to-morrow," Fanny said, after a short pause, "but I can't get anybody to take me."

"Will you permit me that honour," I asked, sotto voce.

"With pleasure," Fanny replied ; "you rink, of course ? Now really, no prevarication this time, sir."

"Of course," I replied proudly, and felt as dull as dishwater the next moment, for never had a pair of skates been bound to my feet, and Plimpton and I were utter strangers.

"I'm so glad," Fanny cried. "Will you call at eleven."

"I will not be a moment late," I vowed.

"That is right, and I will have mamma ready too," Fanny said, giving me a delighted little tap with that fatal fan.

"Oh !" I returned, and my spirits went down to zero ; "does your mamma rink ?"

"Oh dear, yes," Fanny exclaimed, "mamma is quite an adept. She has had only four falls, but I regret to say that the gentleman who waltzed with her the first time was severely injured—broke his collar-bone."

"Oh !" I muttered, and made an inward vow not to put my precious self in danger's way.

I went home, but not to bed.

What had I done ? Promised to harness my feet to wheels and glide about on a floor as smooth and slippery as a looking glass.

"Oh ! fool," I cried, tearing my hair, "what is to be done ? I cannot retract. She will laugh at me and so will that she-dragon."

I rushed to my book-case and sought madly for a work on skating ; I found one and read it through and through, and then sought my couch in a much easier state of mind.

I dreamt of Fanny, and I dreamt of her fan. I thought it hovered over me like some gigantic bat, and banged me most unmercifully with its wings. Then I was on the Rink astonishing all beholders, and awoke at last to find myself floundering on the floor.

The fatal time drew nigh, and I approached the house which sheltered my beloved Fanny with hesitating and reluctant footsteps.

I was in for it now, and there was no turning back, and ten minutes later found me escorting the Lovelaces, mother and daughter, on the way to the Rink.

We entered, and the ladies were first fitted with skates, and then my unlucky self.

I shall never forget the sensation if I live for a thousand years.

I tried to stand upright and found myself staring at the ornamental ceiling.

Happily this mishap was not perceived, as Fanny and her mamma were reading the band programme, and doubtless arranging further misery for me.

I rose and smiled like a martyr at the stake.

The attendant grinned, and buried his head amongst a pile of Plimpton's patents. Oh! what would I not have given to have had those things off my feet; how I would have kicked that grinning man.

"Come along, Mr. Jackson," Fanny cried.

"I'm coming," said I, faintly, and feeling as if somebody had dropped an icicle down my back; "but really I don't think these skates suit me."

"What is the matter with them?" my charmer asked, and I heard her give a mischievous little giggle behind her fan.

"I don't exactly know," I stammered, but they won't keep still."

"A very common fault with all wheeled skates," Fanny replied. "Come, sir, we are waiting for you."

I gave one glance of despair round that Rink teeming with ladies skimming about like nymphs, and then made a wild dash towards the spot where Fanny and her mamma stood waiting for me.

I felt myself going, going, and like an auctioneer selling his own property, was knocking myself down.

Crash!

The back of my head felt hot, and a numbing pain shot through my frame, and it is my firm belief that elbows, knees, and head came in contact with the merciless asphalte at the same time.

"Accidents will happen," exclaimed a merry voice, and I took my eyes from the chandelier and beheld Fanny bending over my prostrate form.

"Give me your hand, Mr. Jackson. I hope you are not hurt."

"She stoops to conquer," observed a dandy, and sniggered at his own joke.

I glanced unutterable things at him, but he did not seem to be at all impressed or disturbed, and I came to the conclusion that my orbs had lost the lustre that was wont to awe a disorderly concourse into submission.

I rose with aching and trembling limbs, and clung to Fanny with all the desperation of a drowning man clutching at a straw, and she, sweet darling murmured words of consolation in my ear, and advised vinegar and brown paper.

Mrs. Lovelace deliberately sneered at me, and there was no more wretched being on the face of the earth than I.

"Dear me," Fanny cried suddenly, "I have dropped my fan, Mr. Jackson——"

"Oh! certainly," I exclaimed in a shaky voice, and bent down to grasp the pretty toy.

When I say that I stood on my head I do not exaggerate; my feet flew up and I heard a crushing sound as my hat gave way under my weight and shut out my vision. Laughter rang in my ears, and my blood boiled in my veins, and snatching off my damaged chapeau I readjusted it on my diminished head and again sallied forth on my wild career. Talk of Mazeppa on the wild horse of Tartary; you should have seen me bound and helpless on Plimpton's Patent. No acrobat ever contorted his body as I did on that memorable occasion, and a conger eel might have lashed his tail with envy as I wriggled, and writhed over the smooth surface of the asphalte. How many times I fell will never be recorded by me, for at that time my mind was not in a fit state for mental arithmetic, but countless bruises testified how I had fought the battles and with what success.

I floundered after Fanny, clutching at iron columns and dashing wildly against innocent and unsuspecting rinkers whom I floored by the dozen. I struggled madly to keep my equilibrium, and as surely came to grief; I waved my arms about, danced like a restive horse and rasped nose, chin and knuckles against brick walls, and finally found myself sitting down, staring, gasping at the laughing throng.

The last straw had been added to my back and hot and angry I tore off my wheeled tormentors and, retired into a dark corner to rub those partswhere I was hurt most.

O! Plimpton, I forgive you; if you could but see those bruises, I am sure your heart would be touched.

Mark what followed.

I could not find Fanny, I could not find her mamma, and I was much too sore and brokenhearted to go in search of them, and I crawled home as full of pain and misery as ever did a poor racked wretch fling himself moaning on his pallet of straw.

"A letter and parcel for you, sir," said my landlady.

I took them, glancing at the handwriting, wondering from whom they came.

I burst the seal, and my hair stood on end as I read,—

"Miss Fanny presents her compliments to Mr. Jackson and sends him a small token in the form of a fan as a memento of his first appearance on any rink. Miss F. thinks it advisable to tell Mr. J. that when determined to make himself ridiculous he will oblige by seeking out some partner who will appreciate the joke, and not a lady who knows how to discriminate between a gentleman and a fool."

Padded rooms and straight jackets! this was a pretty thing to send to me. Where is the man who dares to utter or write such things concerning my noble self.

Bring him for'ard, and I will carry out the threat once made by Mr. F.'s aunt, and "chuck him out of the winder."

N.B.—There is a white silk fan over my fireplace. Will any young lady have mercy on me and take it down.

MARK TWAIN.

HOW HE EDITED AN AGRICULTURAL PAPER.

MARK TWAIN says—I did not take the temporary editorship of an agricultural paper without misgivings. Neither would a landsman take command of a ship without misgivings. But I was in circumstances that made the salary an object. The regular editor of the paper was

MY FEET FLEW UP.

going out for a holiday, and I accepted the terms he offered and took his place.

The sensation of being at work again was luxurious, and I wrought all the week with unflagging pleasure. We went to press, and I waited a day, with some solicitude, to see whether my effort was going to attract any notice. As I left the office, toward sundown, a group of men and boys at the foot of the stairs dispersed with one impulse, and gave me passageway, and I heard one of them say:

"That's him!

I was naturally pleased by this incident. The next morning I found a similar group at the foot of the stairs, scattering couples and individuals, standing here and there in the street, and over the way, watching me with interest. The group separated and fell back as I approached, and I heard a man say:

"Look at his eye '

I pretended not to observe the notice I was attracting, but secretly I was pleased with it, and was purposing to write an account of it to my aunt.

I went up the short flight of stairs and heard cheery voices and a ringing laugh as I drew near the door, which I opened, and caught a glimpse

FELL HEAVILY ON MY BACK.

of two young rural-looking men, whose faces blanched and lengthened when they saw me, and then they both plunged through the window with a great crash.

I was surprised.

I SAT DOWN WITH MORE FORCE THAN DIGNITY.

In about half an hour an old gentleman, with a flowing beard and a fine but rather austere face, entered, and sat down at my invitation.

He seemed to have something on his mind; he took off his hat and set it on the floor, and got out of it a red silk handkerchief and a copy of our paper.

He put the paper in his lap, and, while he polished his spectacles with his handkerchief, he said,

"Are you the new editor?"

I said I was.

"Have you ever edited an agricultural paper before?"

"No," said I, "this is my first attempt."

"Very likely. Have you had any experience in agriculture practically?"

"No, I believe I have not."

"Some instinct told me so," said the old gen-

MY LEGS SPREAD OUT.

tleman, putting on his spectacles and looking over them with asperity, while he folded his paper into a convenient shape. "I wish to read you what must have made me have that instinct. It was this editorial. Listen and see if it was you that wrote it:

"Turnips should never be pulled; it injures them. It is much better to send a boy up and let him shake the tree."

"Now, what do you think of that?—for I really suppose you wrote it."

"Think of it? Why, I think it is good—I think it is sense. I have no doubt that every year millions and millions of bushels of turnips are spoiled in this township alone by being pulled in half ripe condition, when if they had sent a boy up to shake the tree——"

"Shake your grandmother! Turnips don't grow on trees!"

"Oh, they don't, hey? Well, who said they did? The language was intended to be figurative—wholly figurative. Anybody that knows anything will know that I meant the boy would shake the vine."

Then this old person got up and tore his paper all into small shreds, and stamped on them, and broke several things with his cane, and said I did not know so much as a cow; and then went out and banged

BENIFICIAL RESULT OF RINKING

To BE BOUGHT CHEAP

THE ONLY EMPLOYMENT LEFT.

the door after him; and, in short, acted in such a way that I fancied he was displeased about something.

But not knowing what the trouble was, I could not be of any help to him.

GAZED AT THE ROOF.

Pretty soon after this, a long, cadaverous creature, with lanky locks hanging down to his shoulders, and a week's stubble bristling from the hills and valleys of his face, darted within the door and halted motionless, with finger on lip, and head and body bent in listening attitude.

Still he listened.

No sound.

Then he turned the key in the door, and came elaborately tip-toeing towards me till he was within long reaching distance of me, when he stopped, and after scanning my face with intense interest awhile, drew a folded copy of our paper from his bosom, and said:

"There, you wrote that. Read it to me quick—relieve me—I suffer."

I read as follows, and as the sentences fell from my lips I could see the relief come. I could see the drawn muscles relax, and the anxiety go out of the face, and rest and peace steal over the features like the merciful moonlight over a desolate landscape.

"The guano is a fine bird; but great care is necessary in rearing it. It should not be imported earlier than June or later than September. In the winter it should be kept in a warm place, where it can hatch out its young.

"It is evident that we are to have a backward season for grain. Therefore, it will be well for the farmer to begin setting out his cornstalks, and planting his buckwheat cakes in July instead of August.

"Concerning the pumpkin—this berry is a favourite with the natives of the interior of New England, who prefer it to the gooseberry for the making of fruit-cake, and who likewise give it the preference over the raspberry for feeding cows, as being more filling and fully as satisfying. The pumpkin is the only esculent of the orange family that will thrive in the North, except the gourd, and one or two varieties of the squash. But the custom of planting it in the front yard with the shrubbery is fast going out of vogue, for it is now generally conceded that the pumpkin as a shade-tree is a failure.

"Now, as the warm weather approaches, and the ganders began to spawn ——"

The excited listener sprang toward me to shake hands and said:

"There, there, that will do. I know I am all right now, because you have read it just as I did, word for word. But, stranger, when I first read it this morning, I said to myself, 'I never, never believed it before, notwithstanding my friends kept me under watch so strict, but now I believe I *am* crazy,' and with that I fetched a howl that you might have heard two miles, and started out to kill somebody, because, you know, I knew it would come to that sooner or later, and so I might as well begin. I read one paragraph over again, so as to be certain, and then I burned my house down and started. I have crippled several people, and have got one fellow up a tree, where I can get him if I want him. But I thought that I would call in here as I passed along, and make the thing perfectly certain; and now it *is* certain, and I tell you it is lucky for the chap that is in the tree. I should have killed him, sure as I went back. Good-by, sir—good-by; you have taken a great load off my mind. My reason had stood the strain of one of your agricultural articles, and I know that nothing can ever unseat it now. *Good-by, sir.*"

I felt a little uncomfortable about the cripplings and arson this person had been entertaining himself with, for I could not help feeling remotely accessory to them. But the thoughts were quickly banished, for the regular editor walked in. (I thought to myself, "Now, if you had gone to Egypt, as I recommended you to, I might have had a chance to get my hand in, but you wouldn't do it, and here you are, I sort of expected you.")

The editor was looking sad, and perplexed, and dejected.

He surveyed the wreck which the old rioter and these two young farmers had made, and then said:—

"This is a sad business—a very sad business.

There is the mucillage-bottle broken, and six panes of glass, and a spittoon, and two candlesticks. But that is not the worst. The reputation of the paper is injured permanently, I fear. True, there never was such a call for the paper before, and it never sold such a large edition or soared to such celebrity; but does one want to be famous for lunacy, and prosper upon the infirmities of his mind? My friend, as I am an honest man, the street out here is full of people, and others are roosting on the fence, waiting to get a glimpse of you, because they think you are crazy. And well they might after reading your editorials! They are a disgrace to journalism. Why, what put it into your head that you could edit a paper of this nature? You do not seem to know the first rudiments of agriculture. You speak of a furrow and a harrow as being the same thing; you talk of the moulting season for cows, and you recommend the domestication of the polecat on account of its playfulness and its excellence as a ratter. Your remarks that clams will lie quiet if music be played to them was superfluous —entirely superfluous. Nothing disturbs clams. Clams *always* lie quiet. Clams care nothing whatever about music. And, heavens and earth! friend, if you had made the acquiring of ignorance the study of your life, you could not have graduated with higher honour than you could to-day. I never saw anything like it. Your observations of the horse-chestnut as an article of commerce steadily gaining in favour is simply calculated to destroy this journal. I want you to throw up your situation and go. I want no more holiday—I could not enjoy it if I had it. Certainly not with you in my chair. I would always stand in dread of what you might be going to recommend next. It makes me lose all patience every time I think of your discussing oyster-beds under the head of 'Landscape Gardening.' I want you to go. Nothing on earth could persuade me to take another holiday. Oh, why didn't you *tell* me you didn't know anything about agriculture?'

"Tell you! it's the first time I ever heard such an unfeeling remark. I have been in the editorial business going on fourteen years, and it is the first time I ever heard of a man's having to know anything in order to edit a newspaper. Who reviews the books? People who never wrote one. Who criticizes the Indian campaigns? Gentlemen who do not know a war-whoop from a wigwam. Who writes the temperance appeals and clamour about the flowing bowls! Folks who will never draw another sober breath till they draw it in the grave. But I have done my duty. I said I could make your paper of interest to all classes, and I have. I said I could run your circulation up to 20,000 copies, and if I had had two more weeks I'd have done it. You are the loser by this rupture, not me. Goodbye."

I then left.

PETER SIMPLE IN THE ARMY;

OR, TWENTY-FOUR HOURS SOLDIERING.

BY GEORGE EMMETT.

"I'VE had enough of this," said Peter, "I'll go and enlist."

When Peter Simple said "enough of this," he meant it, and that phrase was very expressive of his state of mind at the moment.

The "this," that Peter had had enough of, was a tremendous "tanning" at the hands of Doctor Martimus Blewberry, proprietor of Bombshell Academy, not many miles distant from the historical town of Canterbury.

Doctor Blewberry claimed to be a descendant of the famous Duke of Wellington, and, being in consequence, as he maintained, of military extraction, and being obliged to support his family by schoolkeeping, he adopted the above-mentioned military cognomen for his scholastic establishment in honour of his great relation—as being symbolical of the manner in which the Duke always burst amongst and scattered the enemy.

Peter Simple claimed to be a descendant of the Peter Simple whose sayings and doings have been immortalized by the renowned Captain Marryat.

Peter Simple's father and Doctor Blewberry were great friends, and that's how it was that Peter was sent to Bombshell Academy.

What had Peter done to get a thrashing?

It so happened that Peter, to put it as mildly as possible, was a very pliable, yielding, good-natured boy—a boy, not exactly strong-minded, and, therefore, easily led and persuaded.

Of these characteristics, Peter's school-fellows, who were not such good boys as Peter, took advantage, and were always setting him on to do all kinds of tricks, for which the innocent minded Peter always got a good thrashing.

Each time Peter was thrashed, he called himself a fool, and declared that he wouldn't let his schoolfellows persuade him into doing another trick.

But somehow, when the trial came, Peter's determination was always overcome, and he did the trick, and got his thrashing.

The trick for which Peter was last thrashed, was for putting a soup plate, filled with cold water in Doctor Blewberry's bed.

The Doctor was suffering with lumbago, and Peter had been persuaded to place the plate of cold water in the bed for the Doctor to sit in, as a means of drawing the pain from the Doctor's back.

But, as it happened to be winter, the remedy was very objectionable to the Doctor, and who, ascertaining that it was, as usual, "that silly Peter" who had done it, gave him, as usual, a good thrashing, and further, made Peter sit in a plate of cold water all night, to draw the pain from *his* back.

Was it any wonder that Peter had exclaimed, "I've had enough of this! I'll go and enlist?"

Then Peter waited his opportunity, and ran away to go for a soldier.

As being a descendant of Peter Simple, our Peter ought, to have been consistent, run away to sea.

But Peter didn't like the sea.

He had once been persuaded to go on a river in a boat, but his persuaders had rocked the boat so much on purpose that Peter had been made quite sick, and then he thought he should never like the sea.

Peter had not many miles to go and, in the course of three hours, he came to the gate of Canterbury barracks.

At the gate, marching up and down, with his spurs jingling, heavy top boots over his trousers, white gauntlets on his hands, a carbine a scarlet coat, a pouch and belt across his shoulder, a tall hairy hat on his head, and wearing a tremendous black moustache, was a tall Scot's Grey.

Peter didn't know what regiment he belonged to, but he thought the Grey the biggest, most tremendous-looking soldier he had ever seen.

"I'm afraid I'm not tall enough for *his* regiment," thought Peter.

Scarcely had the thought passed through his mind, when the Grey, noticing Peter's earnest look, said:—

"Well, my chicken, what do you want, eh?"

"Please, sir," said Peter, "I want to enlist."

"Oh, that's it, is it, eh?" said the Grey gravely and, as Peter thought, dryly.

"Yes, please, sir," replied Peter.

At this moment, a little soldier, with a trumpet in his hand, came out of the guard-room.

"Here, trumpeter," said the Grey with a wink, "here's a gentleman wants to enlist."

"Ah, what regiment would you like to join, sir?" asked the trumpeter, politely.

"I don't know, sir," said Peter; "I ain't particular."

"That's the style; would you like to be a trumpeter?"

"I think I should," said Peter.

"Well, let's test you. Have you got all your teeth?"

"Yes, sir."

"Open your mouth. No you hav'n't," said the trumpeter, "there's one wants cutting. Did you feel that?"

This question was caused by the trumpeter having thrust the mouth-piece of his trumpet in Peter's mouth.

"Ah—h—ah—O—o—o—h—O—o—oh, myth—loo—loo—O—o—o—oh—loo—haf—hurth meth!" mumbled Peter, holding his hand to his mouth, twisting about with pain, and looking at the trumpeter with tears in his eyes, "Wha—wath—loo—do—lath for?"

"To cut the tooth, of course. You can't enlist unless you have all your teeth. Have you good eyesight?" asked the trumpeter, whilst the Scots Grey stood by with his sides shaking with suppressed laughter.

"I—I—think tho," said Peter, who could not yet speak plainly.

"What can you see?" asked the trumpeter, suddenly striking Peter in the left eye with his fist. "Sparks, blue red, and gold coloured, and all that, eh?"

"Ye—ye—yeth," returned Peter, quickly removing his hand from his mouth to his eye. "I—I—thay—don't do thath. I—I—can thee without thath." Peter had not yet got back his speech.

"HERE, TRUMPETER," SAID THE SCOTS GREY, "HERE'S A YOUNG GENTLEMAN WANTS TO ENLIST."

"Must do everything that's right," said the trumpeter, winking at the Grey and several other big Greys who had come out of the guard-room. "You want to enlist, don't you?"

"Yes, sir."

"Very well, then. Can you hear a loud noise well?"

"I think so, sir," putting his hands up to his ears and shrinking back, as though anticipating an attack.

"Let me see if you can hear this," said the trumpeter. "Take away your hands. I'm not going to hurt you. That's it. Now."

Peter having taken down his hands, the trumpeter put the bell of his trumpet to Peter's ear, and blew a blast that made our candidate for the army fancy his brain had been stunned by an awful clap of thunder, and that the drum of his ear had been split.

So long did the humming and ringing sensations last, that Peter began to think they would never subside, and he staggered about and looked at the trumpeter in such an odd, idiotic manner, that the latter began to exhibit symptoms of a convulsive nature.

Presently overcoming these symptoms, the trumpeter resumed his examination of Peter.

"You still wish to enlist?"

"I—I—think so, sir," said Peter, in a less confident tone than he used at first.

"Then we must see if you are tall enough. We must put you in the gauge. Come this way. Some one lend us a hand," added the trumpeter, winking at the group of grinning Greys.

Standing near the gate was a large cannon, with a bore of large calibre.

To this the trumpeter conducted Peter, followed by a big Grey.

"Lay hold of him," said the trumpeter.

The next instant, before Peter could offer a protest, he was lifted up, and his head was actually in the muzzle of the gun, and he felt himself being forced in.

"Oh! oh! don't!" cried Peter, in a tone that sounded hollow and sepulchral. "I—I—shall be smothered!"

But Peter felt himself still being pushed up the cannon, and his sensations were dreadful.

We cannot describe them, but recommend a practical test to our readers.

Presently Peter's head was stopped by the breech—he had been "rammed home" as a gunner would say—and the next moment Peter felt something pricking the back of his head, and so painful was it, that Peter, as well as he could, began to sing out.

The wicked trumpeter had put a "pricker" through the vent of the gun, and pricked Peter's head, as though it had been nothing else than a cartridge.

This gauging ordeal, however, did not last long.

Though it seemed countless ages to Peter, not more than half a minute had elapsed from the moment his head went in the muzzle, till Peter himself was brought to daylight.

As Peter sat on the ground rubbing the back of his head with tears in his eyes, his face and clothes covered with black dirt—for he had cleaned the gun quite as effectually as a sponge—he looked an object for pity, but his appearance elicited roars of laughter.

Never before had the great Scots Greys laughed so much.

"I think you'll do for a trumpeter," said the trumpeter. "It isn't everybody will come up to the gauge."

"But what did you prick my head for?" asked Peter.

"To see that it wasn't soft. We never have soft-headed trumpeters—it wouldn't pay,"—winking again at the Greys. "Do you still wish to enlist?"

Peter had now begun to think that going for a soldier was almost as bad as being thrashed by Doctor Blewbury, but he didn't like to show the white feather.

"Yes, please," said Peter.

"Then come along with me."

The trumpeter, bestowing a parting wink on the laughing Greys, led the way to the barrack-rooms.

As they were passing through the square, the trumpeter was accosted by a big soldier, whose jacket sleeves and other parts were decorated with gold lace.

He was the great Sergeant-major of the Greys.

"Who have you got there, trumpeter Cod?" asked the Sergeant-major in an abrupt manner.

"A mouse,* sir,"—demurely.

"Oh! don't come it too strong—d'ye hear?"

"Yes, Sir."

"What does he mean by 'don't come it too strong?'" asked Peter, as he followed the trumpeter into a barrack-room.

"He means that we're not to put on too much soft soap."

"What do you put on soft soap for?"

"To get you clean for passing the doctor."

"But I am clean," said Peter. "I have a bath nearly every day!"

"Well, we shall see presently," returned the trumpeter. "This is a barrack-room. I'll introduce you to my chums. Here, chums,' added Cod, addressing two boys who were sitting at a table soaking some "Tommy" in basins of tea; "allow me to introduce you to—What's your name? I forgot to ask you before."

"Peter Simple."

"Peter Simple." said Cod. "He's come to enlist"—winking.

"Oh, indeed!" said one.

"Glad to see him," said the other. "Is he all right?"

"I've looked at his teeth," said Cod. "He was one deficient, but I soon cut that for him, It was nearly through. I've tested his left eye. and he saw the proper colours."

"Then I'd better try the right," said the first one (Jack) who had spoken; and before Peter knew where he was, his right eye was, tested in the same manner as the left had been.

Then followed the testing of the right ear, in like manner as the left—by sound of trumpet.

Both these operations, as will be imagined,

THE TROOPER AND THE YOUNGSTER MEASURE PETER.

* Nickname for a Recruit

caused Peter much pain and bewilderment, but the testing process had not yet been finished.

Scarcely had Peter got rid of the rainbow colours from before his right eye, and the humming and drumming from his right ear, when his new testor asked another question.

"Are you sound in the wind Peter," asked Jack.

"I—I—dont know what you mean," replied Peter.

"Sound in the wind—sound just there,"—hitting Peter a tremendous poke below the left ribs, which doubled him up as though he had the cholic. "Ah!" continued Jack, "you're not quite sound I see. But never mind, you'll do so far. You can have some tea now, and after that, you shall see the Doctor."

Cod, and Jack, and the other trumpeter—Bob—were very kind to Peter after the testing.

"You've stood it like a brick," said Cod, and you shall have some of the best of the tea."

"Thank you," said Peter.

"Cook," said Cod, making a telegraphic sign to that individual with his eyelid. "A basin of the best for Peter Simple."

In obedience to this command, the cook took a pint white basin, dipped his ladle in the tea-can, and half filled the basin with tea—extracted tea-leaves.

"There," observed Cod, handing it to Peter. "That't the stuff for you, Peter. Pitch into it."

"But this is only tea-leaves !" said Peter looking blankly at the contents of the basin. "I can't drink tea-leaves !"

"You must eat 'em," said Cod. "Why, they are the best part of the tea ! There's nothing else, and I have given you my share."

Now Peter was very hungry—he had had nothing to eat since he had fled from Bombshell Academy ; but he couldn't get down the tea-leaves.

All Peter could do, was to look mournfully at the basin, and wish he hadn't "gone for a soldier."

The whole affair was very different to what he had expected to find it.

Peter's ideas of a soldier's life had been formed under the enthusiastic representation of Doctor Blewberry.

The Doctor had several times dined at the officer's mess in the barracks, and he had dazzled his boys' imagination by the description of the number of courses, the vast display of silver plate on the mess-table, the gorgeous uniforms of the officers, the brilliant candelabra, and the magnificence and number of the mess waiters.

Peter had an idea that he had only to enlist to enjoy all these luxuries, and he was more than "considerably disappointed" at the meagreness of the food placed before him, and the coarse way in which the soldiers evidently lived.

The barrack-room didn't come up, in any degree, to his fondly imagined expectations.

Instead of a carpeted bedroom, with a snug feather bed, and a nice arrangement of china for ablutionary purposes, here were twenty beds, as narrow as a sofa, in one room, filled with straw, and covered with coarse sheets, blankets, and a common red and white rug for a counterpane, and, as for washing things, why—he couldn't see any !

Big men were lounging about the fire, on the forms and beds, smoking and spitting, passing rude jokes, making use of bad language, and evidently much amused at Peter !

There wasn't even a curtain to one of the windows, and anybody could look in and see what everybody was doing !

The only ornaments in the room were the bright swords, hung to a black wooden beading that passed round the bare whitewashed walls, the carbines in rest, and tall hats, encased in macintosh cloth which stood beside the top-boots with polished spurs, on an iron rack fixed to the four sides, near the ceiling.

There was no cupboard—only a long wooden shelf suspended from the ceiling in the middle of the room !

The fire-irons were so large that Peter felt sure he could hardly lift them, and the coal box was made of cast iron, and large enough to hold half a ton of coal !

Peter didn't like the look of things at all.

"If this is a soldier's life," thought Peter, "I am sure I shall not like it !"

After tea Peter's initiation was resumed.

It was a very short ceremony, however, this time, and the last for the evening.

"You look feverish," said Cod. "Come with me to the doctor, he'll give you something to cool you."

Peter, not knowing whether he was feverish or not, followed Cod into another room, where he was introduced to a personage in a long blue coat all down to his heels, and a hairy hat that seemed almost as big as his whole body.

In this mysterious person's hand was a white basin.

"This is the new recruit, Doctor," said Cod.

"Is he feverish ?" asked the Doctor.

"Very," said Cod.

"Then take this, youngster," said the Doctor, handing Peter the basin, "and go to bed."

"What is it, please?" asked Peter. "Medicine ?"

"Exactly," said the Doctor. "Down with it !" he added sternly, as Peter began to pull a wry face.

Peter would rather not have taken it, but there was no help for it, and Peter swallowed it and went shuddering to bed.

Peter had taken a dose of Epsom salts !

Everything was so strange, and Peter was so

uncomfortable on the straw bed, and was so qualmish with the dose of salts, that it was long after " out lights " before he could go to sleep.

When Peter next awoke, it was with a shock, and a sensation as though he was standing on his head.

And this was a fact.

When Peter had collected his senses, he found that his head was on the ground and his feet in the air.

The head of the iron bedstead had, from some cause—Peter could not make out how, given way in the night.

Peter fancied, however, he heard sounds as of persons tittering, but he hadn't time to make sure on that point, as he suddenly felt very ill, and he was obliged—dressed as he was only in his shirt—to make his way out of the room, if tripping over buckets, tubs, mop and scrubber handles, which seemed to be strewed mysteriously about, can be called making his way.

Peter was so bad that he groaned dreadfully, and moaned out in very lugubrious tones that he wished he hadn't gone for a soldier.

It was a long time before Peter got back to bed, and when there, he laid and cried himself to sleep.

In the morning Peter was roused up, and ordered by Cod to take the tables and forms into the barrack yard, and scrub them white with soap and sand.

Peter pleaded illness as an excuse to be let off the duty, for it was bitterly cold, with an east wind blowing, and the snow falling.

But Cod boxed Peter's ears, and made him do it.

Peter did it, crying all the time, and kept calling himself a fool for ever going for a soldier.

When Peter had finished scrubbing the tables and forms, he had to take them back again, and then he was permitted to have his breakfast, for which meal he again had the best that was going —a piece of stale " tommy " and the richest of the coffee grounds.

Peter ate the bread, but he couldn't manage the coffee grounds.

" Are they too rich for you, Peter?" asked Cod.

" Yes, sir," said Peter, not liking to offend.

" Then go to the pump, and when you return you shall see the Doctor again."

Peter went and had a drink, and, on his return, Cod kept his word, and took Peter to the Doctor —the same who had given him the dose of salts.

" Are you better, Peter?" asked the Doctor, tenderly.

" Yes, sir," replied Peter, who didn't want any more salts.

" That's right. Let me see your hand."

Peter held up his hand, palm upwards.

" Turn up the backs," said the Doctor ; " why you've got the 'scratch,'" he added, as Peter did as he was desired. " You dirty fellow, how dare you come to enlist with the 'scratch?'" Anoint him ! away with you !"

And before Peter had time even to ask what the " scratch " was, he was whisked out of the room, conducted to the private lavatory, stripped and anointed.

The oil with which Peter was anointed, consisted of a " scratch " allaying composition of train oil and soot.

Peter was then ordered to dress in an old uniform provided for him by Cod, and marched back to the barrack room, feeling greasy and gritty, and carrying about with him an unpleasant smell, so that, although everybody laughed at Peter, nobody would go near him.

This happened to be muster day for the troops, and Cod thought he would initiate Peter into his duties.

" Peter," said Cod, " this is the day the men are mustered, and you'd better take a basin and go to the serjeant-major for the mustard."

" Yes, sir," said Peter in a very doleful voice, ' where is the serjeant-major?"

" In the square, walking about. You'll be sure to see him. But, first of all—do you see those boots up there in that corner, with the spurs on ?"

" Yes," said Peter.

" Then, just get them down, and pipeclay the spurs. There is the pipeclay box and sponge in the window."

Peter willing to obey, if only to gain the good will of Cod, took down the boots, and soon had the spurs beautifully whitened.

The boots and spurs belonged to the serjeant in charge of the room, and had been got up extra smart for muster parade.

Just as Peter had finished, the serjeant came in to dress for muster, and when he found what Peter had done, he swore a dozen round oaths, and rung Peter's ears till they were as hot as fire, and red as two round slices of beetroot.

" This is getting worse and worse," said Peter with a sigh that was almost a sob. " Oh, I wish I hadn't gone for a soldier !"

But Peter was not allowed much time to sigh.

" Now take the basin," said Cod, " and go for the mustard."

Peter, scarcely knowing whether he stood on his head or his heels, took a basin and went into the square.

Here Peter felt rather awed, and decidedly ashamed and nervous at the company he found himself in.

Not only was the serjeant-major there, strutting majestically about with a silver-headed whip in his hand, but several officers, and the whole of

SOME PLEASANT SKETCHES FROM PETER SIMPLE'S CAREER IN THE ARMY.

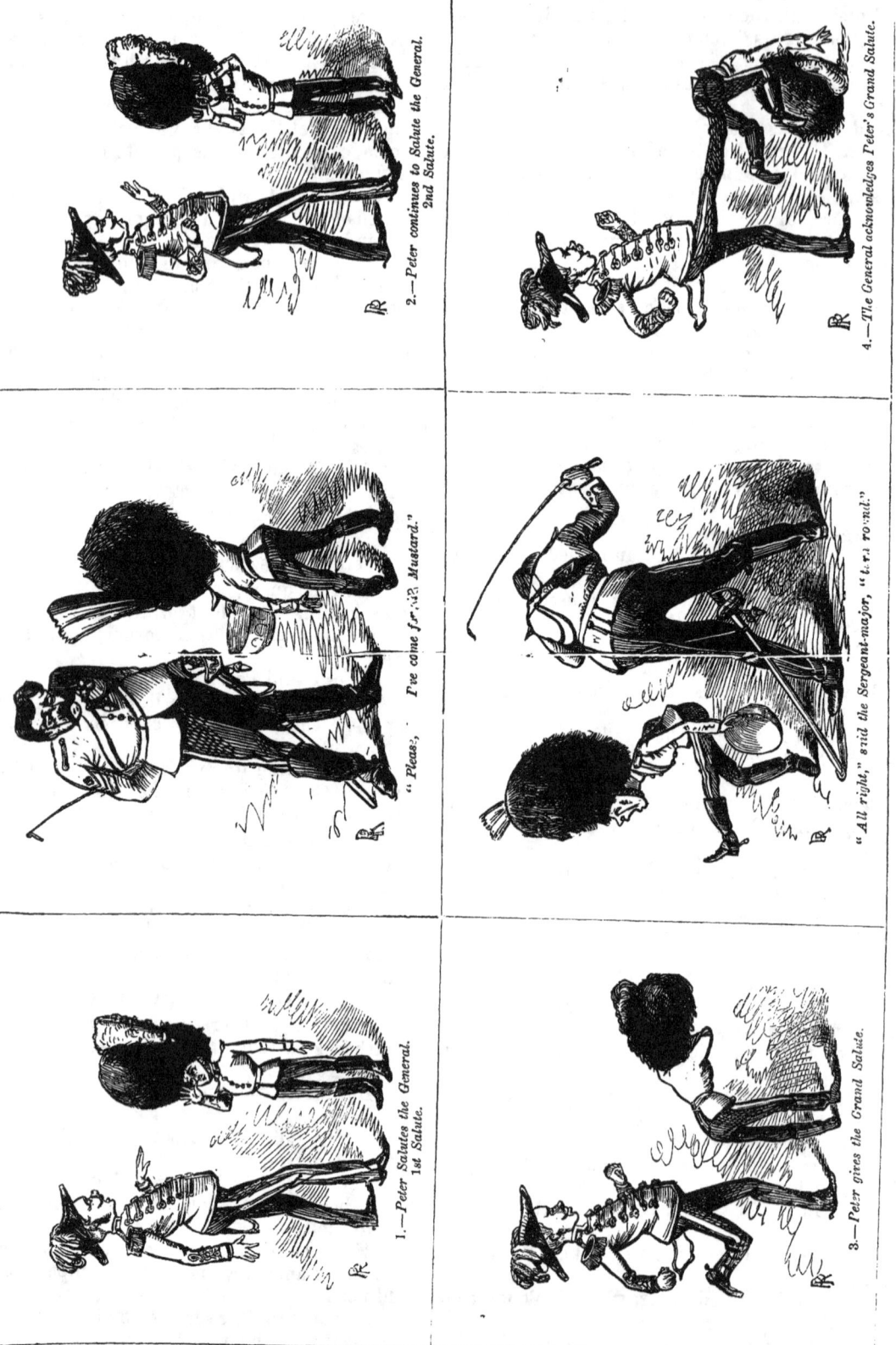

the soldiers, not on duty, in the barracks, waiting to fall in for muster parade.

As Peter approached the serjeant-major, with his black greasy face, and the basin, a general titter went round the soldiers.

"What do you want?" asked the serjeant-major, casting a severe look on Peter.

"Please sir," said Peter, "I've come for the mustard."

A grim smile passed over the serjeant-major's face as he replied—

"All right—turn round."

Whereupon Peter did as he was desired and, the next moment, he let the basin suddenly fall and went howling away, wriggling and holding himself behind.

This was caused by the Serjeant-major's whip falling on Peter's "right-about-face."

"What a fool I was," sobbed Peter, "to go for a soldier!"

There were several other "wrinkles" which Cod and his chums taught Peter that day, but, as we have not space to describe the process of initiation, we must pass them over, and introduce Peter to the reader at dinner-time the following day.

This was Sunday, the room was extra clean and tidy, the dinner was on the table, and the Greys were in full dress, just returned from church, all waiting for the appearance of the General Commanding.

Peter was there in the company of Cod, Jack, and Bob.

"Peter," said Cod, "this being Sunday, the General always comes round the rooms after church, and you, being a new hand, must salute him. It's done in four motions. When the General comes in, you must step up to him and salute with the first motion. You stretch out your arm to its full extent, like this" (showing), "draw it gently in and place your right thumb against the right side of your nose, with the fingers spread out like a fan—so. Then you must pause a moment, and if the General says nothing, you must make the same motion with the left hand. That will be motion number two, and you will have both hands to your nose—like this." (Showing.) "Then," continued Cod, "if the General makes an exclamation, you must immediately turn to the right-about-face, and slowly and gracefully bend your body forward, until your trousers come tight behind. Those will be motions three and four. Understand?"

"Yes," said Peter.

Scarcely had Peter spoken when there came a general rattling of swords and jingling of spurs, and the General, accompanied by at least a dozen officers of various ranks, entered the room.

"'T'shun!" cried the orderly non-commissioned officer.

Peter here felt himself nudged, and heard Cod whisper,—

"Now!"

Shaking very much, and scarcely knowing what he was doing, Peter stepped in front of the General and, extending his right arm, brought his thumb gracefully to the right side of his nose.

At this extraordinary motion, the General looked greatly amazed; but he was more amazed still, as Peter performed motion number two.

"Why—why—what's the meaning of this outrageous ——— ?"

But the General could not finish his speech from sheer dumbfounderment as Peter went to the right-about, and, bending gracefully forward, presented his bent back to the great officer.

Presently, after gazing in wondering silence at Peter's bent rotundity, the General stammered out,—

"Wha—what is the meaning of this?"

"It's a salute, sir," said Peter.

"Salute!" cried the General, sternly. "Then allow me to return it."

The next moment the General's foot was elevated and meeting with Peter's rotundity, sent Peter flying into the fire-place, where he nearly stuck, with his face against the bars.

Ten minutes afterwards Peter was running back to Bombshell Academy, crying,—

"I've had enough of this. I'll go back to school."

If our readers should feel at all interested in Peter Simple, we will chronicle his sayings and doings in a story called, "Peter Simple at Bombshell Academy," and further, in after life, in a story entitled, "Peter Simple in the Army."

Why is a dishonest bankrupt like an honest poor man?—Because both fail to get rich.

Which is the most difficult punctuation?—Putting a stop to a woman's tongue.

Why is a young lady like a bill of exchange?—Because she ought to be settled when she arrives at maturity.

How to make a slow horse fast—Tie him to a post.

When can a lamp be said to be in a bad temper?—When it is put out.

What's the difference between the Khédive of Egypt and a swan's back?—One's hard up and the other's soft down.

In what key would a lover write a proposal of marriage?—Be mine, ah

Why does a coal-barge weigh less than an empty sack?—Because, if the one is a light weight, the other is a lighter.

Why is a pig the most extraordinary animal in creation?—Because you must first kill him and then *cure* him.

ALPHONSO ANSTRUTHER'S AMATEUR THEATRICALS;

OR, THE MISERIES OF MACBETH.

ALPHONSO ANSTRUTHER was highly ambitious to be an actor.

He spouted speeches from Shakspeare: delighted in declaring that his "name was Norval"—which it most certainly was not—and was perpetually viewing an invisible dagger as that treacherous Thane, Macbeth, did, when he did to death the drunken footman and the sleeping Duncan.

Many a time had his spirits been greatly grieved when the committee of the amateur theatrical club to which he belonged announced that Othello was to be sold for a guinea : Iago for fifteen shillings, and Cassio for ten ; for the Kemble Club did not choose their leading people by their fitness for their parts, but the length of their purses, and but too often, the ambitious actor could only afford three-and-six for the Duke.

How he hated little Biggs, the low comedy man of the company, who always had enough money in his pocket to purchase the best parts in the farces, and did make the audience laugh sometimes : when he—Anstruther—could never make them cry.

Biggs laughed at tragedies : said he could not see the use of them—unpoetical beast—declared that it was all nonsense to pay your money to pretend to be miserable, and to make your fellow creatures really so.

In fact, there was no end to Biggs' bad taste, and Alphonso Anstruther always glared at him when they met, and Biggs never lost his temper.

It was, therefore, with no small amount of pride that Alphonso Anstruther strode—he always "strode," never walked : considering the ordinary step far beneath the pace consistent with the dignity of a tragedian—into the committee room of the Kemble Amateur Dramatic Club, and announcing that a distant relation of his had died, bequeathing a small fortune to him, he had determined to take the theatre at Blueclayville for a fortnight, and would engage his company from the lovers of histrionic art to be found in the members of the Kemble Club.

Of course everybody wanted to go, but that was impossible.

Biggs applied for the low comedian's place, but was rejected with scorn.

"All right, Stubbs," said Biggs ; "I'll be equal with you for that."

"Stubbs !" ejaculated Alphonso. "What meanest thou, base-born varlet, by that name ?"

"I mean that I know who you are ; you are Albert Stubbs, whose mother kept a mangle in Providence-place, and that you were educated in a charity school, and that your rich uncle was old Garrett, the penny pieman, in Podger's-rents, down Houndsditch. Oh ! you need not glare at me ; I ain't afraid of you."

"Begone !" screamed Alphonso, "thou art beneath my notice : wretch !"

"Am I beneath your notice !" laughed Biggs. "Well, I will see if I cannot make myself worthy your notice my fine fellow. I am not easily put down, I can assure you."

With that he walked out of the room whistling a comic tune.

And now Anstruther was all powerful.

Everybody in the room condemned Biggs, called his behaviour brutal, and suggested that some one should " punch his head ; " but as Biggs happened to be a man who could box remarkably well, it was thought better to leave him alone.

The pieces were first settled upon. " Box and Cox " first, and Alphonso grinned with delight when he thought how much Biggs would feel at not having his favourite part of "Box" to play. Then was to be performed the tragedy of " Macbeth," Mr. Anstruther taking the part of the treacherous Thane.

This having been settled upon, Mr. Anstruther stood threes of gin warm all round, to drink prosperity to the new venture, told the company what station to start from, and also the date when they were to appear at Blueclayville Theatre.

Rehearsals were declared to be unnecessary, as everybody had acted in the characters assigned to them at least twenty times, and expenses had to be cut down. So it was agreed that they should run over the pieces in the club-room the night before they started to Blueclayville, so as to save hotel-bills.

Nothing could have gone better at the rehearsal.

Every one was dead-letter perfect ; no one missed their entrance cues more than half-a-dozen times, and as for Anstruther, his "Macbeth" was truly terrible.

Off he started for Blueclayville early the next morning, to see that everything was ready at the theatre ; the rest of the company were to follow in the afternoon.

He found the scenes and properties all right at the theatre, but the dresses had not arrived; however, this did not put him out, as he relied upon the costumes coming down with the company.

Which they did; but unfortunately Jones, the low comedian did not arrive; but Biggs did.

"Hillo! Anstruther," cried the abominable little Biggs, "how are you old fellow?"

Anstruther made no reply, but seizing hold of Mr. Greaves who was to play Banquo demanded in a stern whisper.

"Where is Jones: and why have you brought that idiot Biggs with you?"

"I did not bring him: he came by himself," was the reply; "and Jones went out with Biggs on the spree, and the consequence is he cannot lift his head from off his pillow this morning. You know what a terrible bilious fellow he is."

"But who is to play Box," shrieked the unhappy Anstruther.

"I will," said Biggs, coming up similingly; "I know the part by heart."

Anstruther ground his teeth with rage: but what was he to do?

There was no time to send to London for another actor.

Besides, he did not know where to send. Bow-street to be sure is a favourite spot of the gentlemen of the footlights: but how are you to know them from the ordinary mortals, and even if you found them they are not to be engaged at a moment's notice.

With a bad grace Alphonso Anstruther consented to accept Mr. Biggs' offer.

And how Biggs played Box!

The audience roared with laughter, he was so extremely comic.

Anstruther was so vexed that he—being in the front to see the opening farce—hissed. Whereupon a burly dweller of Blueclayville, called him an ass; informed him that he knew nothing of acting and threatened to kick him out of the theatre neck and crop.

He looked as if he meant what he said too: so Alphonso thought it more prudent to express his contempt for the man by silence, and his disapproval of the acting by leaving the theatre.

Then the curtain fell with sounds of applause and mad with envy Anstruther tossed off his clothes and commenced dressing for Macbeth.

But here a most frightful accident was discovered to have happened.

The dresser had brought the Scotch Chieftain's garb perfectly correct with one exception.

He had either mislaid or lost the kilt.

There was the body with its silver buttons, the socks, the broad sword, the target, the shoes and buckles, the tights and plumed bonnet. Everything but the kilt.

Alphonso Anstruther gazed woefully around him.

ALPHONSO ANSTRUTHER AS RICHARD III.

He was not a handsome man, and his legs were somewhat thin.

Biggs said that Anstruther's legs were the finest he had ever seen: in fact had they been a little bit finer no one could have seen them at all: but then Biggs was a scoffer and jealous.

"But what can I do!" demanded Anstruther in tones of misery, but little suited to the gallant Thane of Cawdor, "I can't go on in this state.

There was no doubt about that; commonsense and decency forbade it.

A general consultation took place amongst the actors; but the only suggestion made, viz., that he should play the part in a pair of modern trousers was rejected with scorn.

"If yer please, sir," cried the call-boy, "the second scene is nearly over, and there ain't more nor two witches. Mr. Fothergill, the manager, says he must have another."

"Gracious goodness!" gasped Anstruther, "I had quite forgotten that. It's all that beast Jones's fault; he was to have played the third witch, doubling it with the drunken porter."

"I say, Anstruther," cried Biggs, bolting into the dressing-room, "here's a go! No one to play the third witch."

"I know it, sir," said Anstruther, drawing himself up to his full height, and trying to look dignified, in which proceeding he utterly failed, owing to the incompleteness of his costume. "I am painfully aware of the fact."

"Well, if you like, I will play it for you. I only want a sheet and a clothes prop, I know the part."

Alphonso Anstruther glared with hatred at his tormentor.

He felt convinced that in all these accidents little Biggs was deeply concerned.

"I am much obliged for your offer, Mr. Biggs," he said sternly; "but the curtain must go down."

"Ring the curtain down?" cried little Biggs, "if you do that the people will wrench the seats up."

"But what am I do? I can't play Macbeth in this dress. Who ever heard of Macbeth without a kilt?"

"That is perfectly true," said Biggs in a thoughtful voice; "it could not be done."

"I should think not. But perhaps, Mr. Biggs, *you* have a kilt and would play the part?"

"No, tragedy is not in my line. But I know what to do. Mrs. McTabby, the little dwarf woman who plays the children in the cauldron, has a plaid petticoat that will do. I will get it in a minute. She won't know, for she has taken it off and is dressed as Banquo's son, Fleance. I will be back directly."

"But are you sure she will not know?" gasped Anstruther. "She has such a temper, you know."

"Not she; besides, if she does we must plead necessity. Hark! what a row the people are making."

"I suppose you must," sighed Anstruther, "but it is all very terrible, very terrible indeed."

Away sped Little Biggs on his errand, and soon returned with the plaid petticoat.

"Here you are, Anstruther, my boy," he cried "it don't *quite* match your dress, that being green whilst this is red; but we must not be too particular, you know. Jump in! That's it. Dear me, how tall you are, and how short McTabby must be. Clever little body though; worth her weight in gold at playing children."

"Yes," sighed Anstruther, "she would be all very well if she did not fly into such tempers."

"If you please, sir, the third witch must come," shrieked the shrill tones of the callboy.

"I come, I fly, and will be with you anon," said Biggs, and the next moment he dashed out of the room, with difficulty suppressing his laughter.

And, truth to tell, Anstruther did cut a most comical figure.

BIGGS AS THE FOOL IN HAMLET.

His thin legs came out far beyond his kilt, his boney knees making them look like a pair of tongs, on which a plaid petticoat had been hanged to dry.

Indeed the whole appearance much resembled that useful member of the fireirons family. His Scotch bonnet looking like the flat knob at the top, the handle represented by his long neck, whilst his body stood for the little round joint in the middle.

At last the eventful moment came when he had to enter with his friend Banquo.

The audience laughed a good deal at first, but soon grew used to the grotesque figure, and settled down to witness the performance in a quiet and watchful manner.

All went well.

Anstruther roared and ranted; his was no *fretting* an hour upon the stage, but hard work.

He tore his passions into such rags, that had they been real ones he would have made the fortune of a paper-merchant.

Until the third scene in the first act the audience laughed, but did so quietly.

But here little Biggs got a queer bit of mischief in his head.

The stage directions ran thus—
Scene VII.—Macbeth's Castle.—Hautboys and Torches.

Enter a Sewer (an Officer who serves up a Feast) and divers servants with dishes and services and pass over the stage.

This might have gone all right had it not been that, as the men went over, a small tumbler labelled "whisky" was dragged across by a string running from one side to the other.

"Wretch!" cried the infuriated tragedian, "you have ruined me."

As he spoke he clutched hold of little Biggs who, having dragged the glass over, was drinking the contents.

"Ruined you," cried Biggs; "what do you mean?"

"What do you mean," retorted Anstruther, "by dragging that whisky over the stage?"

"I did not go on to the stage; the audience did not see me," replied Biggs coolly.

"No, sir, but the whisky. You pulled the string that dragged it across."

"Oh! ah! yes, I did that, it was the only way I could carry out the stage directions."

"Directions! what do you mean by that, sir—what do you mean by that "

"Why it says, 'enter a sewer.' Well, as I could not get a 'sewer' I tried a *little drain.*"

Mr. Anstruther gnashed his teeth, but the audience were impatient at the stage wait, and he had to rush on and commence his celebrated speech of—

"If it were done when 'tis done, then 'twere well,
It were done quickly."

amidst the roars of the audience and the titters of the actors, who had heard the joke.

Once more the piece dragged on its weary way undisturbed until the first scene in the second act, and then, when Macbeth says to the servant :—

"Go bid thy mistress, when my drink is ready,
She strike upon the bell."

Some wretched fellow in the gallery exclaimed :—

"What, more whisky? You will be tight before the play is half over."

"Hurrah!" cried some one in pit, "give us a comic song and a toast after your grog, old fellow."

"Willie brewed a Peck o' Malt!" was suggested by another.

"And dance the Highland Fling," shouted a fourth, "*do* let us be cheerful."

"Ladies and gentlemen—gentlemen and ladies, I implore you not to spoil the 'great bard's' best play."

"We can't," yelled a little brute of a boy, "you have done it already for us."

Alphonso Anstruther groaned a deep groan, and shivered in his kilt with rage.

"This—this—this is a conspiracy," he gasped, "a vile plot."

"We know it is. You and your old woman have planned to murder the gent as took too much for supper," shouted the fiend-like boy who sat in front of the gallery. "We knows all about it, don't we, old man?"

The last part of this speech was addressed to a fellow-joker in the pit, who replied surlily,—

"I don't know nothing about it. I thought it was the piece which they was a-murdering of."

"Gentlemen," appealed Anstruther, "I appeal to your generosity. I am a *h*aspirant."

"So its seems, by the way you put on that 'H,'" roared a fellow from the pit.

Poor Anstruther grieved at this more than anything, for he knew to make an error in grammar was an actor's worst fault.

"I beg pardon, I am sure," said the unhappy man; "but if you will let me proceed I will try to do better."

The appeal was so humble that the audience burst into a shriek of laughter, and granted it.

Then in deep tragic accents Mr. Alphonso Anstruther began again—

"Is this a dagger that I see before me?
The handle toward my hand. Come, let me clutch thee!"

Scarcely had he said the last words before a fine full-roed red herring fell from the flies, and hung suspended before his nose.

Vainly did he try to shove away or catch the strongly flavoured, rather common, but succulent fish.

It was certainly a novel sight to see Macbeth playing "cherrybob" with a bloater all over the stage.

"Go it, Mac!" shouted the boys in the gallery, who had now become so familiar with the Thane that it ought to have bred contempt, but he was too crestfallen for fine feelings.

"Go it, Mac! Well done, bloater! Nearly had him then, 'Beth, old boy! Try again. If you don't at first succeed, try, try, try again."

And the burden of that once popular melody smote upon Macbeth's ears, a death knell to his hopes.

Seeing his trouble, Lady Macbeth hurried on to the stage and commenced speaking.

"Lose no time, my lord, but haste thee to do the deed that shall make us both—"

Here she uttered a yell of agony, for in his attempt to catch the bloater he had shot it in her eye.

"Oh, my eye! my eye! my eye!" screamed the lady.

"I go, and it is done!" shouted Macbeth; and rushed off the stage.

And then the red herring, as if making a bow to the audience, wobbled about and was hauled up into the flies.

From this time the audience seemed only watching for mistakes.

For instance; when Macbeth exclaimed, "This is a sorry sight!" some one replied, "You are, old man."

And when he looked at his blood-stained hands, the fiendish boy in the gallery called out—

"That comes of meddling with red herrings. It's the blood*ed* of the bloat*er.*"

Thinking to correct this error as to where the blood came from, Alphonso put in this line—

"'Tis old King Duncan's blood; I slew him in his bed."

"No you did not; he was slewed before he went there, and is now at the Crown smoking his pipe and drinking fourpenny."

Again, when he held his hands to his face and shuddered, the fiend-boy shouted,—

"Oh, crikey! don't he shiver at the smell o' bloater'! P'raps it wasn't a fresh one."

And so the performance went one, until it came to the celebrated Witch Scene.

This was very well rendered, with the music as well, so that the audience became quieter.

Biggs, as the third witch, was the biggest success, he having danced so well.

Then Macbeth came in, and the audience had become so used to his figure that they did not laugh so much.

Thus encouraged, Anstruther proceeded much more evenly, and hoped to redeem his lost laurels: not even despairing when some one suggested "black pudding," for the sow's blood mentioned as one of the ingredients of the cauldron.

Then the armed head arose out of the cauldron, delivering its warning in such expressive tones, that the audience applauded, and Anstruther's hopes ran high. After this came Mrs. McTabby, as the apparition of a child.

In shrill querulous tones she gave out her first line—"Macbeth! Macbeth! Macbeth!" and in harsh tones did that gentleman assure her that, had he been blest with three ears instead of two, he would have heard her—a statement not much to be wondered at.

But what was Macbeth's horror when "the child" stretched forth its skinny arms and shrieked—

"Oh you wretch! you thief, you've got on my petticoats, give them to me at once."

"For heaven's sake, Mrs. McTabby, go on," pleaded Macbeth, "you shall have them when the piece is over."

"I'll have them now," cried the lady, commencing to crawl out of the cauldron.

"But nonsense, my dear Mrs. McTabby: you can't want them now," argued Alphonso Anstruther.

"I say I do want them Mr. Anstruther, and what's more, I *will* have them, there now.

"But I can't take them off on the stage? Consider the audience wouldn't like it."

"Yes we should—we should—we should," shouted the pit and gallery in chorus.

"Give the girl her petticoats," screamed the fiend boy. "Oh, you wicked old man to steal a girl's clothes."

"For mercy's sake: don't, Mrs. McTabby, don't," screamed Anstruther, "consider the madness."

"You should have considered that at first," said Mrs. McTabby, dashing after Macbeth like a fury.

But Macbeth's legs were long, and he managed to escape from her clutches, and to dodge her round the cauldron, and in and out between the three witches, who were convulsed with laughter at his capers.

The more he doubled and ran, the more little McTabby screamed and pursued.

"Save me, save me, save me?" roared Anstruther, "she will kill me, I know she will."

"Give it to him, little 'un," yelled the fiend boy, "don't knock under, but have your clothes."

Mr. Alphonso Anstruther stumbled and would have pitched on his nose, but Mrs. McTabby at that moment seized him from behind, and literally began fighting with tooth and nail till the Thane roared again.

In his fright poor Anstruther stamped on the third witch's little toe, who immediately shoved him back with violence.

Unfortunately for Mrs. McTabby she was standing with her back to the cauldron, facing Anstruther's back, so that as that gentleman staggered back she did the same, and finally, both fell backwards into the witches' stew-pan.

Now the reader must know that theatrical cauldrons are made without bottoms, so that the spectres or phantoms may arise through the trap in the stage, and thence through the cauldron, so that they may appear to be really brewed out of the devil's broth.

This being the case, Mrs. McTabby vanished first, and then Anstruther, shutting himself up in the shape of a V, disappeared afterwards, whilst the stage carpenter entering into the joke, lit a quantity of red and green fire.

"Hillo!" roared the fiend boy. "Here's old Macbeth gone to blazes before his time."

"Bravo! bravo! encore! encore!" shouted the audience.

"Let's have it again."

"Let's send the witches arter him," shouted the fiend boy.

"Hurrah! hurrah!" screamed the rest, and immediately there was a rush for the stage.

"Ring down the curtain!" shouted the witches to the prompter. "Ring it down at once."

But the warning came too late: the audience were on the stage, and the witches flew for dear life.

Biggs escaped by the window, and having fled down two or three streets, entered a shop and bought a new hat, that being the only thing he had lost, he having played the witch's part in his own clothes, with only a sheet over all.

This done, he lit his cigar, and humming a tune, walked quietly to the railway station.

He had just reached the gates when a figure half-clad as a Highlander and half as an acrobat, fled past him, and hurrying up to the booking-office, demanded a ticket for London.

It was Alphonso Anstruther, and that was the last seen or heard of Macbeth and his miseries.

What vegetable is anything but agreeable on board ship?—A leek.

What is the difference between a tradesman who uses false weights and a highwayman?—The tradesman lies in weight, while the highwayman lies in wait.

Why is every teacher of music necessarily a good teacher?—Because he is a sound instructor.

PHILANDER JACKSON V. CORNELIUS DABBER.

THIS is an action that is to come off very shortly—that is to say, as soon as the necessary funds can be raised, against Cornelius Dabber for libel against our old friend Jackson, and this is how it all came about.

For a long time Dabber has been quietly but persistently slandering and libeling Mr. Jackson

As Mr. Justice Mellor very truly observes, " A

The cashier carefully looked the other wa while the sub-publishers grinned and muttered together, the only words Philander was able to make out being " Prigging checks."

" Very strange," thought he to himself. I suppose somebody has been getting into trouble ; however, we shall soon see.

On his entry into the editor's sanctum, a rough copy of the " Comic Annual " was put into his hands in silence ; while what might be termed a

OH, BATHOS ! DABBER WAS ASLEEP.

man may overlook one or two attacks, and then a third might put his back up."

This is the present case : for a long time Dabber has been writing what he pleased, and, mistaking contempt for fear, has been making each attack stronger than the former.

At length Mr. Jackson determined that upon the next attack he would take measures for clearing his character.

The time came sooner than was expected.

One morning, last week, when Mr. Philander Jackson made his appearance at the office, there seemed to be a certain something in the air that he could not understand.

The office boy was grinning audibly ; the publisher acknowledged his " Good morning" with a supercilious nod.

stifled giggle, rose from the corner where the sub-editor was working.

Scarcely had Jackson cast his eyes over the book ere the colour began to rise in his expressive features, his hair 'gan to twist and stand upright, like quills on the fretful author, while his inward emotion found vent in a gurgling grunt.

He had fallen upon Dabber's Introduction ! ! !

" Where is he ? " Lead me to him ! Shew me the traitor ! " burst from his lips in a succession of shrieks.

The editor was about to observe something which from the dignity expressed on his face, would not have been very palatable to his hearer when he suddenly stopped.

A peculiar "tip, top, hop and go one " became audible.

Somebody was coming up the passage to the office.

"Here he is," exclaimed the Sub-Editor. "Hurrah! won't there be a row."

Philander Jackson became very pale, and the next moment the door opened and Dabber made his appearance.

"Good morn——" began the ancient mariner when he caught sight of Jackson, with the annual in his hand.

The excitement displayed in the slandered one's face, betrayed that he had discovered all, so Dabber had nothing to do but to grin and bear it.

Calmly taking a chair, he observed,—

"Hallo! You don't look quite the thing. Wot's hup?"

For three minutes Jackson could not speak; he drew his chair close to Dabber's, and in vain he endeavoured to articulate.

All at once the impediment gave way, and his wrath burst forth.

With full dramatic action he read what he termed "the disgusting libel," and then he informed his hearer that at length his patience was used up, no longer {would he allow it to pass by, the law of the land should take it up, and the—the—vile, virulent villain, who had worked all this evil, should receive his reward.

Then he looked up, to see what effect his eloquence had had upon the libeller.

Oh, Bathos! Dabber was asleep!!!

After this, you cannot be surprised that Mr. Jackson is only waiting for the subscriptions to pour in, to file his bill, and commence his case against the slanderer.

PHILANDER JACKSON, H.U.A.

Why is one who has solved an enigma like a superannuated carpenter?—Because he has explained

MR. MIGGS' MISERY.

A RAMBLING STORY.

SOME people—foolish, ignorant ones—declare that men take to street-tumbling, organ-grinding, Punch-and-Judying, and such like professions for the sake of idleness.

All I can say on that matter is this—let them try it.

I've been a Punch and Judy man now nigh upon thirty years, and my experience goes as far as this —carrying a Punch and Judy show all over England and Wales ain't a cheerful occupation, and is calculated to break one's back and spirits at the same time.

Did I ever have a show of my own? No, never.

I never could raise the money for that.

But I was very near upon inheriting one once.

How was that!

Well, I don't mind telling you, only talking is dry work.

Thank you; I don't mind if I do have another glass. Mary, my dear, a warm "squeez;" you know, the pure, pelucid juice of the juniper; one lump of sugar, a dash of hot water, and a thin piece of lemon-peel.

Ha! God bless the ingenious gentleman as gave us gin; it's all very well for them preacher chaps to call it a "curse," and may be they're right; but let them try a cold night, rags for clothes, no shoes, and an empty stomach, and see if they won't enjoy a drop of Old Tom.

Well; but you were asking me to tell you how I nearly became a manager, and I've been rambling off all about the juniper juice; but I can't help it, I'm given to rambling, I suppose it comes from having been on the tramp so much.

But here goes for the story, and no flies.

I had been a clerk in an office in the City, only a junior one, you know.

I used to sweep out the office, and run errands, and keep the postage stamps.

My master chose at last to say that I *did* keep the postage stamps a great deal too much; but lor', there was no truth in the assertion.

He gave me in charge, but I was let off without a stain on my character; but *he* would not give me a character or take me back again.

So then I was turned adrift on the world, with no one to pity me or take the slightest interest in me.

Innocent! Aye, as innocent as the babe unborn, but what was the good of me saying that. Give a dog a bad name and you may as well hang him, and that's an old saying. There's Toby over there—one-eyed Toby—lor' sir, that dog got a bad name and lost his eye through it.

How was that?

Why it happened in this way.

You see sir that dog got a bad name in a model lodging house; people lost their herrings and haddocks, and all was put down to Toby.

Now Toby you see has a tremendous amount of curiosity.

That's the way he has picked up so much knowledge, sir.

All clever men must be curious; if they were not they would not know a thing. You see a fool goes about staring at everything, and seeing nothing, but a fellow who has his head screwed on the right way, he notes down everything, and if he don't quite understand a thing he asks questions until he does.

Well, sir, Toby happened to be looking very inquiringly into a cupboard where Mrs. Todgers, the landlady, kept her cold victuals. I think he wanted to find out what the family had had for dinner. But everybody had said that Toby was a thief, and of course Mrs. Todgers put his curiosity down to an attempt to steal, so she heaved a bundle of wood at Toby and pricked out his eye.

Yes Toby, good dog; that's how you lost your blinker.

But there I go rambling away again, and I was going to tell you how I became a Punch and Judy man.

Well sir, I sank lower and lower down in the world until I was pretty nigh starving, when it happened that I fell in with one Sam Slokum, who was the proprietor of a Punch and Judy show.

Sam was in a deuce of a fix, because his partner, as was, had thrown up the Punch and started a phantochine show.

Sam was a good one at the mouth organ and drum, having a natural taste for music, but he could not do the "roo-to-too-to-too" of Punch.

He was always a trying at it, always; but it was no go. But rum and water had spoiled his voice, and when he put on the squeak he was about as musical as a Cochin China cock with a cough.

Now *I* took to it natural; I could sing Tommy Dod right away all through in Punch's voice, and so Sam Slokum offered me an engagement, and that's how I got into the line.

But, unfortunately, just before I settled with Sam a gentleman lost his purse, and I found it.

Accident! Of course it was: only it looked suspicious. So much so that I determined to go off into the country with Sam at once, so that I should not have to answer impertinent questions.

Unfortunately I told Sam this, and from that moment he became a perfect tyrant. He would never take the show for a minute; but used to walk along by my side, blowing miserable notes out of his pipes, now hitting the drum, and then me: and drumsticks hurt, I can tell yer.

"Sam," I used to say, "I won't stand it, there now; if you don't put that stick down, I'll strike."

"All right my beauty," replied Sam, giving me an awful cut with the stick, "if you can strike, so can I. You turn rusty, and I shall wop you first, and then hand you over to the tender mercies of the police!"

Then he would start blowing on his pipes :—

"If I had a donkey wot wouldn't go,
Wouldn't I wollop him? Oh no, no."

With one drumstick he beat the drum, and ith the other me.

I suppose it was being so badly treated when I was young, that made me submit: but submit I did, and Sam, who was naturally of a miserable turn of mind, seemed to take a delight in crushing me down.

He used to love to dilate upon the pains of prison—he had been there once or twice—and to hear him describe the treadmill would make one's flesh creep.

Well, I got crushed down, and at last became quite in his power. I found that he was not altogether a bad fellow when he kept away from rum, which he never did whilst he had a halfpenny in the world.

Well, we started on our rounds as usual, striking up northwards.

But business was bad, and Sam Slokum had changed much for the worse.

I think the bull must have shaken his intellect, he grew so miserable.

It was a terribly wet season, and we had just left the cathedral town of York, and had got out on a plain. One of those long dreary tracks of country as don't have an object to break the monotonous line to the eye.

"Sam," says I, "look here for a moment, and don't play the Hallelujah chorus on those pipes and drum; they ain't instruments suited to it."

"I've been looking all round," said I, "and I don't see ne'er a house or a village where we can put up at, let alone try our luck with the show."

Sam hit the drum a awfu. wop and wailed on his pipes.

"What is to be done now?" I continued. "I'm shivering with cold and am as empty as your drum."

Here Sam rubbed the head of the drum stick over the parchment of the drum, which makes a very unpleasant noise to a man as is hungry.

"For mercy's sake, Sam, don't do that," I said, "but do answer a fellow."

"William," he said, after a pause, "I feel as 'ow I've done my last."

"Done your last!" I exclaimed. "What do you mean?"

"I mean that I'm going to tramp out of the world, William. I've done with tramping through it. Let me sit down at the foot of that tree, and you pitch the show here and play to me."

"Nonsense, Sam," says I, "it ain't so bad as all that comes to, is it?"

"It is, William, I feel I'm at my latter end," said Sam, seating himself at the foot of the tree. "So, William, let me see the show once more, and then I shall die in peace."

Well, sir, I did pitch the show, and as I pulled the green baize curtain round me I couldn't help sobbing.

However, I went to work, and I did my best performances, Sam beating the drum, blowing faintly at his pipes, and looking on with a mournful gaze.

At last the performance was over, Sam joined chorus in the last root-ti-too-ti-too, and then I stepped from behind the curtain.

"William," said Sam, mournfully, "you can't do the root-ti-too-ti-too as you used. You ain't got the same mellifluous squeak you had in days gone by."

"I've done my best, Sam, I replied, "no one can do more."

"True, William, true; but did you hear that boy in the last village as we passed through give the call—the one as stood a pint of beer to me?"

"I heard him," said I, "he did do it as good as a professional."

That *youth* will be a profession, William, mark my words about that, he will be."

"Then I pity him," was my reply.

"Don't say that, William, don't say that; that lad's voice is a fortune. But there, I haven't time to look at them things, William, my time 'as come, we must part."

"But you can't die here, Sam, said I, sobbing.

"Can't I William, I should like to see whose to prevent me. Look here, William, when I am dead you must take the show. You have been very faithful to me, very, and I have no one else to leave it to. So when I am no more the show is yours."

I squeezed his hand, but could not speak, for I was sorry, sir, very sorry.

You see we had not been great chums; but we had been a good many years together, and had got used to one another.

"Now, William," he said, "just put the Punch, and the Judy, and the rest of the Company on that box, so as I can see them, and then go to the village, which is just three miles from here in a straight line north, and fetch a doctor and some one to help me."

"I'll run all the way," I cried; "but you can't be so near your end as that?"

"William," he said, "it is born in upon me. You won't find me here when you come back, hurry as you will. Now go."

Well sir, I hurried off as fast as I could, and when I got a long way from Sam I heard him shout out: Roo-te-too-ti-too much better than he had ever been able to do it before. So I guessed it was all up with him as I had heard somewhere that people at the last moment often have their intellect brighten up, just as a candle brightens up afore it goes out.

So I hurried along mapping out my plans, and determing to lay by money, for the Punch and Judy business is not so bad after all if you are careful; but Sam used to spend all his money on rum.

Now, I like gin,

Take another glass?

Well, since you are so pressing I don't mind if I do.

The same as before Mary, with just the least bit more lemon-peel.

At last I reached the village and I went straight to the doctor, and he called the constable and the constable took two men with him, to carry Sam back to the village.

The doctor was a tall peppery man, who looked daggers at me although he did not say much.

Thinks I to myself, if your physic is as nasty as your look, I am glad I am not your patient, and Sam will have had a lucky escape if he dies without your assistance.

We went over the fields the constable swearing —the doctor frowning, and I thinking that Sam was not the cruel wretch I had considered him after all.

At last we arrived at the field, and I looked around everywhere for Sam and the show.

There was the tree sure enough, but the show and Sam had gone !!!

"Where is the dying man," demanded the doctor angrily.

I—I'm sure I dont know sir," stammered I, "I left him at the foot of that tree."

"But you told me he was dying," roared the doctor.

"And so he told me," I replied. I don't understand it at all."

The constable looked at the doctor, and the doctor at the constable.

They at first thought I was a raving madman, and perhaps I should have been taken back to the village and kindly treated, but here my usual luck stepped in, and one of the men exclaimed:—

"I knows what it is, doctor. This be first of April and he be making on us fools."

Vainly I protested that such was not the case.

the tooting of the Pandean pipes, mingled with the well-known cry of Punch.

I thrust my way through the crowd, and stood face to face with Sam Slokum.

I flew at his throat.

Sam sprang back and in doing so upset the show, and I saw the youth whom Slokum had declared would enter the profession rolling in the mud.

In a minute I saw through all that had occurred.

Sam Slokum had pretended to be dying, having engaged the village youth who did the rooti-tootitoo so beautifully to take my place.

that I had left Sam Slokum dying beneath the tree.

The doctor kicked me, the constable and the men chased me until I fell into a ditch or horse-pond, I don't know which; all I do know is that when I came out I looked as if I had been taking a bath in a pot of green paint.

At last I escaped from my tormentors and hurried south as fast as I could.

It was about the end of March that I crawled into London, and footsore and weary I crept along the streets.

I had just reached the Archway Tavern, Highgate, when I heard the beating of a drum and

He had sent me off for a doctor and had then signalled for that youth, and this was the call I heard so plaintively on the breeze.

Sam dared not lock me up, and so I walked off followed by my only friend, Dog Toby.

You see I've got known down here at the theatre and they give me odd jobs as super, and I runs out to get the actors' beer, and so forth.

As for Toby he has no end of friends.

The girls in the ballet, God bless them all, feed blind Toby.

But I must be off home now.

Well, sir, I don't mind just another glass to wash down my miseries.

DABBER AMONG THE SPIRITS.

By THE SUB-EDITOR.

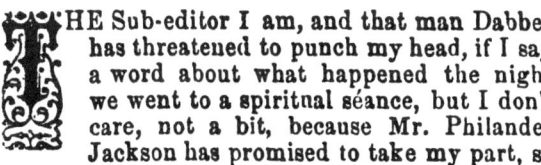

THE Sub-editor I am, and that man Dabber has threatened to punch my head, if I say a word about what happened the night we went to a spiritual séance, but I don't care, not a bit, because Mr. Philander Jackson has promised to take my part, so if the one-legged old humbug tries any of his little games on with me, he'll find himself in the wrong box.

Who's afraid! I'm not, so here goes.

It wasn't very long ago that I had an invitation to attend a circle of "investigation," not fifty miles from Bloomsbury.

I was alone in the office, and had just pulled out the letter to see at what time I had to be there, when in walks Dabber in his usual cheeky familiar manner.

"Hullo, messmate," said he, "what have yer got there, a paper for the theatre?"

"No," answered I foolishly, "It's an invite to a spirit meeting."

"The deuce it his," said Dabber, "I'm hon, it's bound to hadmit two, and I'm hawful fond of spirits."

"But this is a séance," I replied; "a circle, don't you understand?"

"Don't care ha bit ole feller," answered the old villain with a smack of the lips. "I'd jest has soon drink 'em out of a sayonce as not, or in a circle, or a square, or anything, it don't matter to me."

"But this is another kind of spirit, Dabber," I continued, trying to make him understand; "It isn't rum."

"Jest the thing, dear boy," he persisted. "I'm only too glad to get a chance of tasting a noo spirit, I'm tired of the old 'uns."

"But I havn't an invite for you," said I, falling back upon my last resource. "How can I take you without an invitation."

"Pooh, pooh," replied the conceited old image, "jest you sen' up word to say that you've brot Dabber with you, and you'll fin' there'll be no difficulty made, only too glad to git me ole man, it's a fac."

And so I was obliged to consent to take him with me.

In the meantime he pulled out a dirty, short, black, clay pipe, as strong as a sewer, and cadging some 'bacca off me, he began to smoke, stinking the office out and nearly choking me, until I was quite glad when I'd finished what I was doing, and could get up to leave. When we got

ALL THE FUN OF THE FAIR.

outside Dabber said:—

"Ole man, you may as well 'ave two-pennyworth, now we're hout."

Thanking him for his offer, I agreed, and we adjourned to a neighbouring tavern.

I had a glass of ale, and Dabber had some hot rum. As soon as he had drank his down, he said—

"This bar his too 'ot for me, Tom; I'll wait for yer houtside."

And then he went out and left me to pay for the drinks!

I gave it him well when I got outside, but Lord, he didn't care.

"Orl rite ole man, keep yer wul on," said he. "We'll make it rite when we get to this spirit store of your'n."

And forced to be content with this, away we walked I was going to say, but "stumped" is the better word, up Fleet-street.

Presently I began to see that, (as Dabber walked so slowly) at the pace we were going we should be late.

I mentioned this to my companion, who at once suggested—

"Take a 'ansom, Tom, take a 'ansom."

"Will you pay half, Dabber, if we do?" I enquired?

"In corse I'll do wots right and proper, and pay my share. 'Oner, Tom, 'oner."

Relying upon his honour to pay half the fare I called a hansom cab, and directed the man where to drive to. Going up towards Holborn we came to a street just covered with stones, over which the cabman walked his horse.

This, however, didn't suit Dabber—

"This is orl 'umbug," said he. "We ain't a-goin' to pay for this."

So saying he stretched out his wooden leg over the dashboard in front, and commenced prodding the horse in his hinder parts.

The animal which seemed a nice easy going nag, naturally enough objected to this, and putting his head down between his front legs, he began kicking away with his hinder ones, at a most furious rate.

Then I saw another specimen of the ancient mariner's character, turning very pale and trembling visibly, he said, "I didn't mean to 'urt 'im, do let me get out, I'll never do hit again."

However, when the horse had kicked away for about five minutes, and nearly smashed in the front of the cab, he got tired of it, and consented to continue his journey.

In a short time we arrived at our destination, and holding out ninepence, I said—

"Now then, Mr. Dabber, where is your half?"

First of all he felt in one pocket, and then in another, until he had been all round; and then looking as innocent as a kid he said,—

"Well hi never, hi must 'ave bin and left my puss at 'ome Tom, hi must owe it to yer my boy, hi'll pay yer hon Saterday."

And so I was done out of my cab fare, eighteenpence, but never again, Dabber, never again—

Knocking at the door, in a few moments a servant opened it, and in reply to my enquiry,

She showed us into a sitting room.

Here I introduced Dabber as a friend of mine, and a literary gentleman; I was quite ashamed to do it, but of course necessity has no law.

As soon as he was introduced the Medium, who acted as master of the ceremonies, said—

"I am glad you have arrived, as we were on'y waiting for you to complete our circle; your friend, too, will be a welcome addition, as one gentleman is unable to attend."

Then we all sat down round a table, and placing our hands upon it so that everybody's hands touched those of his neighbour, thus forming a continuous chain, which is the great art of Spiritualism, we waited. Presently the Medium looked over towards Dabber, and said—

"Are you a believer in Spirits, Sir, or an outsider?"

Dabber looked anxiously at him for a moment, as if expecting the offer of a glass of grog, and then he replied—

"Hive bin a berleever in Sperits for nigh upon sixty eres."

"Dear me," answered the other, with an expression of astonishment. "I was not aware that our tenets had been promulgated so long ago as that."

"Oh, yes, hindeed," said Dabber, "hive allers stuck to it, there's nothink like sperits, bere's all very well, and so his wine, but sperits his the best."

Fortunately somebody had a fit of coughing during the latter portion of the old sailor's speech, and so that nobody heard it but myself.

When we had been waiting patiently for nearly twenty minutes, I noticed that Dabber began to fidget about on his chair, as if he was not quite happy.

Glance after glance he threw at me, as if begging me to do something for him, but as I am not acquainted with the language of the eyes I could only sit still and wonder what was coming.

All at once Dabber jumped up.

"I ax yer parding," said he, "but hi ad sum sorlt fish for dinner, and hi'm that dry, hi must go and get a glarse of water."

The Medium wished to ring the bell, but Dabber wouldn't hear of it, and saying he should be back immediately, he stumped out of the room.

He was not gone more than ten minutes, and from the way in which he wiped his lips with the back of his hand on his return, I imagine he had not confined himself to cold water.

When he came back to the table he pulled his chair in next to me, which, as I am not partial to the smell of rum, I was not grateful for.

Soon after Dabber's return to the room, it was proposed that the gas should be put out, and that we should have a "dark séance."

This was agreed to, and in a few minutes we were all in the dark.

We had not been five minutes thus, before I felt Dabber take away his hand from mine, and from the rustling I could tell that he was feeling in his pocket.

While I was wondering what the meaning of this could be, for I well knew that Dabber was not in the habit of indulging in such luxuries as pocket-handkerchiefs, a peculiar sound became perceptible.

Gluck !

Gluck ! !

Gluck ! ! !

Gluck ! ! ! !

"Hark !" exclaimed the Medium, "the spirits have entered the circle."

Gluck !

Gluck ! !

Gluck ! ! !

Gluck ! ! ! !

Another rustle, and Dabber's hand came back to mine.

"Look, my friends ! Behold !" exclaimed the Medium in a voice of rapture. "Behold ! there is a spirit light !"

I had joined the séance in a spirit of investigation, so when I heard this, I looked all around to endeavour and discover this ethereal light.

For a few minutes my search was in vain, and then all at once I saw something close to me that exhibited a phosphorescent gleam.

For a moment I was wonder-struck, and was unable to move hand or foot.

Then suddenly making up my mind to test this light, and see what it was composed of, I raised my hand ; and passing it over towards this mysterious gleam, opened it widely, and pouncing upon it, seized hold of Dabber's nose.

It is a fact. The amount of alcohol that man has drunk during his life has given his nose the property of a stick of phosphorus.

Of course, when I found out what I had got hold of, I begged his pardon, and let go.

Shortly after this we again heard that mysterious—

Gluck !

Gluck ! !

Gluck ! ! !

Gluck ! ! ! !

It seemed strange to me that this noise should always be accompanied by the absence of Dabber's hand from mine.

So the next time we heard the peculiar sound I began to feel carefully round, and just caught, Cornelius in the act of returning a big pint bottle to his pocket.

The old rascal had taken the opportunity when he was out of the room, of obtaining a bottle of his favourite spirit—rum.

All at once we heard a sharp, well-defined "rap, rap," which appeared to come from the middle of the table.

"At length," exclaimed the Medium. "I thought we should not wait altogether in vain. Who are you?" continued he.

"Nelsing," replied a hoarse voice, somewhat resembling a nutmeg-grater being rubbed along a brick wall.

"Are you happy ?"

"In corse hi am."

"When you were dying in the arms of Captain Hardy——"

"It's a lie ! Hi died hin the arms hov Dabber."

"Dear me, how very emphatic these sailor spirits are." exclaimed the Medium. "I was certainly under the impression that Captain Hardy was the one ; however, it is better not to irritate the spirits, so I won't contradict him."

After this there was a lot more knocking, and, to confess the truth, I began to feel just a leetle nervous, when suddenly a lump of wood came down "bump" upon my toe, and I recognized Dabber's wooden leg.

Putting my lips close to his ear, I whispered :—

"Is that you, that was knocking, Dabber ?"

"Itsh shall 'rite ole mansh," replied the mariner in a maudlin tone of voice. "Itsh shore 'rite, itsh Nelsing, don't maksh noish."

Then his head fell back, and from his stertorous breathing I could tell he had fallen asleep.

During this time the Medium was waiting very patiently for further manifestations.

"It's never of any use, my friends, to endeavous to force the spirits," observed the Medium. "If they do not choose to come and be interviewed we cannot make them, and sometimes I have known them get into furious tempers when it has been tried. But, hark ! What is that ?"

A deep heavy rolling sound was plainly audible, sounding like miniature thunder.

Silence was dominant for a few minutes, while we all listened eagerly to the mysterious noise.

"The spirits are angry," remarked the Medium, "and we had better postpone any further investigations to another evening."

So saying, he struck a match and relit the gas.

My first object of remark was my neighbour Dabber.

With his head leaning against the back of his chair, his nose fiery red, and his mouth open, he lay fast asleep, while most portentous snores were escaping from his nasal organ.

And now for a bit of open confession.

I don't suppose I ought to have done it, but the temptation was too great to be resisted.

I took my scarf pin, and ran about three-quarters of an inch into that part of the body Dabber generally uses for sitting upon.

With a stifled shriek, the drunken old humbug sprang to his feet.

But having only one to land upon, he rocked, tottered, and fell full length upon the floor.

By the time he had regained his feet, my pin was replaced in the scarf, and 'twas in vain that he endeavoured to pump me as to the cause of his sudden awakening.

Shortly after this, everybody commenced leaving, and after thanking the Medium, who had endeavoured to lay open the mysteries of nature for our benefit, I also left, still accompanied by Dabber.

"Givsh me yer armsh, ole man," said the mariner, when we got outside.

Accordingly, I lent him the aid of my arm, and well it was for him he had it.

Have you, gentle reader, ever seen a cracker flying and bounding about, all over the place? Well, Dabber was a species of human cracker.

First, he would bounce up against a lamp-post, and then he would drag me forcibly against somebody's doorstep.

At length, crossing Long Acre, the climax occurred.

At the corner of a

street stood a quiet, sober-looking constable.

Our route took us past this man, and just as we came opposite him, Dabber turned round, and resting against me, stuck his wooden leg with all his force in the active and intelligent officer's stomach.

The policeman went over like a nine-pin, and then Dabber tried to run.

In three minutes he was in custody on the way to Bow-street.

I followed, hoping I might be of some service, but directly the In-

spector saw him, he cried "What, here again : lock him up!" and he was taken off to the cell, where he remained all night.

The next day it was "forty shillings or a month."

Of course, Mr. George Emmett was applied to, and foolishly enough, in my opinion, he paid the fine.

I've no doubt Dabber will try and deny all this, but I have related nothing but facts, so I ain't afraid of Dabber or anyone else.

[THE SUB-EDITOR

London : Printed by WOODFALL and K ..... Lane, Strand, W.C.; and Published by GEORGE EMMETT, at ..... t. Bride's, London, E.C.